This edition published by Parragon Books Ltd
in 2018 and distributed by

Parragon Inc.
440 Park Avenue South, 13th Floor
New York, NY 10016
www.parragon.com

Designed by Amy McHugh
Cover created by Comicup Studio—
pencil by Angel Rodriguez, and color by Gloria Caballe

ISBN 978-1-5270-0945-5
Printed in China

Friendship
Task Trouble

Bath · New York · Cologne · Melbourne · Delhi
Hong Kong · Shenzhen · Singapore

One mane-ificent morning in the Castle of Friendship, Starlight Glimmer was practicing spells with Twilight Sparkle.

"Teleportation, multiple locations," ordered Twilight.

ZAP! Starlight speedily changed places several times.

"Transfiguration," said Twilight.

ZAP! Starlight transformed objects around the room.

"Shields," said Twilight.

Starlight made a shield so powerful that it exploded and knocked all the books off the library shelves!

Starlight had done great, though there was some mess to magically clean up.

"Amazing work!" said Twilight. "I have to go out now, but I want you to do some friendship lessons while I'm away."

"Um . . . are you sure?" said Starlight. She suddenly seemed a lot less confident.

"Positive," Twilight replied. "I'll check up on your progress when I get back."

Starlight decided to plan her friendship lessons to show off how clever she was at magic.

"I'll bake a cake with Pinkie Pie and do some scrapbooking with Applejack, sew with Rarity, and help an animal with Fluttershy. Oh, and I'll chillax with Rainbow Dash, whatever *that* is. My trick will be that I do them all at the same time! That'll really impress Twilight," she said.

"I think maybe you're missing the point . . ." said Spike, but Starlight wasn't listening.

So Starlight gathered her friends together. "We'll do everything at the same time to finish fast," she announced.

"Are you sure that's what Twilight wants?" asked Applejack.

"Of course," said Starlight. "Pinkie Pie, you go to the kitchen to bake. Rarity and Applejack, you can both head into the library. Fluttershy, you and your animals can be in the entry hall. Rainbow Dash, please find a room in the castle for chillaxing."

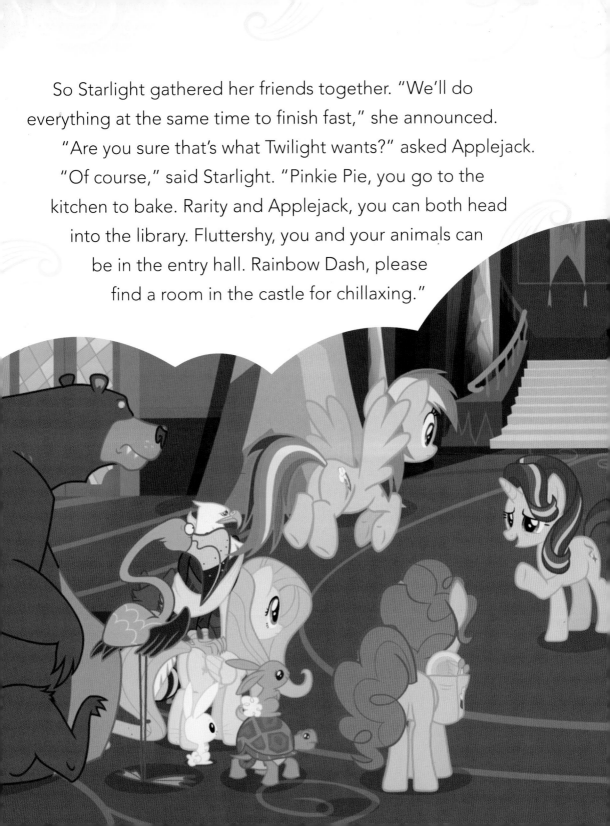

"But the library is far too dusty for sewing. I'd rather be in the entry hall," said Rarity.

"And some of the animals won't be happy here," added Fluttershy. "The eagle might be better in the tower, and the chipmunks would prefer a little nook somewhere."

"I don't think there's anywhere good for chillaxing in the castle," said Rainbow Dash.

"This is taking forever and
we're on a schedule," Starlight muttered
to herself. "I'll use spells to help things along."
She quickly made a clever spell plan and used it on her friends.

"Cogeria . . . Persuadere . . . Fiducia! Ponies, hear my voice
and listen!"

The spells put Starlight's friends totally under her control.

"That's much better," said Starlight. "Now I can
get things done."

She began by taking Pinkie Pie to the kitchen.

"What shall we bake first?" Starlight asked.

"Whatever you want," replied Pinkie Pie, sounding somewhat like a robot.

"Er . . . okay. Well, follow the instructions in the recipe book," Starlight said, before rushing off to the library to see Rarity.

"Make a dress exactly like that one," she said, pointing to a picture.

"Exactly like that one," Rarity murmured, hypnotized by Starlight's spell.

Applejack sat with lots of family photos in front of her, waiting to put them in her scrapbook.

"What do you want me to do?" she asked Starlight in a robotic voice.

"Tell me all about this one," replied Starlight, picking up a photo. So Applejack began to drone on, telling her an endless story about every detail of the photo.

"Er . . . I'll be back in a moment to hear more," said Starlight, then she escaped to check on Fluttershy.

The animals had wandered off while Fluttershy stood like a statue, waiting for orders.

"Why didn't you stop them?" asked Starlight.

"Because you didn't ask me to," replied Fluttershy.

"Obviously I wanted you to! Oh, never mind," sighed Starlight. "Can you please round up all of the animals in the castle and bring them back here?"

"All of the animals . . . got it!" said Fluttershy.

Starlight rushed back to the library, where Applejack was doing exactly what she'd been ordered to do. On and on she droned, telling Starlight in great detail about every single photo.

Then Rarity came over. "I finished the dress. Isn't it gorgeous? It's exactly like the picture," she said.

She was right about that. It *was* a picture!

"I meant make it out of fabric!" Starlight groaned.

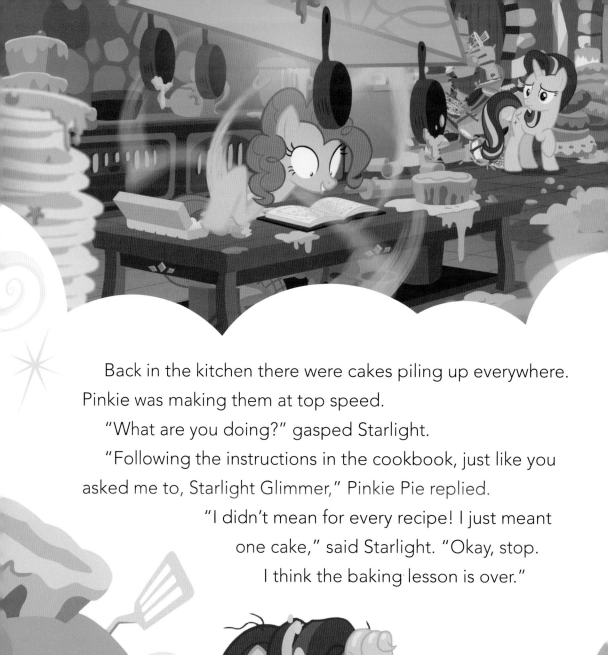

Back in the kitchen there were cakes piling up everywhere. Pinkie was making them at top speed.

"What are you doing?" gasped Starlight.

"Following the instructions in the cookbook, just like you asked me to, Starlight Glimmer," Pinkie Pie replied.

"I didn't mean for every recipe! I just meant one cake," said Starlight. "Okay, stop. I think the baking lesson is over."

Things were not going smoothly, but Starlight wasn't about to give up. She raced back to the entry hall to find Fluttershy surrounded by spiders, beetles, and all sorts of wiggly creepy-crawlies!

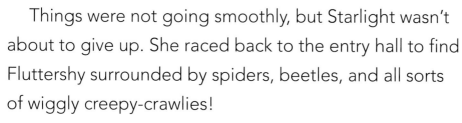

"I gathered up all of the animals in the castle, just like you asked me to, Starlight Glimmer," Fluttershy said, as spiders swung from her mane. There was even a castle rat sitting on her head!

"I can handle this!" Starlight told herself, trying not to panic. "It's just magic, and I'm good at magic."

But there was no time to think of any spells. Before she could do anything, the room began to fill with smoke.

"The cakes are burning. You didn't tell anyone to turn the ovens off," said Pinkie Pie as the smoke began to drift through the whole castle. Things were getting really serious.

"Oh no! We need water!" said Starlight.

"Yes, Starlight Glimmer," Rainbow Dash replied, and instantly made storm clouds appear. Rain pelted down and floodwater quickly began rising in the castle rooms. Luckily, the water flowed out of the windows, but it left lots of puddles behind.

"This just can't get any worse!" groaned Starlight.

Just then, Twilight Sparkle and Spike marched through the front door.

"What is going on?" said Twilight.

She quickly used her magic to untangle Starlight's spells, then she sent the bewildered friends home.

"The spell you used on them was really powerful. They're all going to have headaches in the morning," she warned Starlight. "How in the name of Celestia did things go so wrong?" It was time for an explanation.

"Maybe it would have been better if I had done the spells differently," Starlight wondered, looking through her spell book.

"No it would not have been better! What made you think that casting a spell on your friends to do your bidding was even remotely a good idea?" replied Twilight.

"I don't understand," said Twilight. "You've been so good at all your lessons. Why did this one go so badly?"

It was time for Starlight Glimmer to admit how she really felt.

"I didn't want to fail," she said sadly. "I don't know how to do things like baking or sewing and I was worried I would be a disappointment to you. That's why I used magic on my friends."

"The friendship lessons aren't about how well you can bake a cake or make a dress," said Twilight. "They're about getting to know your friends better by sharing time with them."

"You were right all along, Spike. I did miss the point," Starlight admitted.

"Well, now it's time for a pretty advanced friendship lesson . . . it's called apologizing," said Twilight.

Starlight found her friends sitting at the Ponyville café, nursing throbbing heads and complaining about what had happened.

"Could everypony speak in a whisper?" asked Rarity. "My head is thumping!"

"I burned a cake! I never burn cakes!" said Pinkie Pie.

"I was up all night calming down the animals," added an exhausted Fluttershy.

Starlight said sorry to everypony.
"I messed up," she said. "I cast
a spell because I was nervous
about my friendship lessons."

"Well, here's a friendship
lesson for ya. Don't cast
spells on your friends!"
said Rainbow Dash.

"What I did was wrong,"
said Starlight. "I just hope that
I can make it up to you."

Once Starlight had gone, her friends talked over what she'd said. "That was a pretty good apology," they agreed, and between them they decided to help Starlight clean up the castle.

"I'll rescue the animals," said Fluttershy.

"I'll rescue some fabric," said Rarity.

"And I'll get those storm clouds out of the bathroom," added Rainbow Dash. "Let's go!"

Starlight's friends got busy, and she helped them as best she could.

First, she helped Rarity to repair and hang up the castle wall-hangings. Then she sat organizing photos with Applejack and helped Fluttershy to put the castle's little critters back safely in nooks and crannies.

Finally, she helped Pinkie Pie to do some baking, and even made her friend laugh by getting cake batter on her face.

At last, the castle was back in shape, and so were the friendships. "I think you've nearly completed your friendship lessons after all," Twilight Sparkle laughed. "You and your friends did a great cleanup job together. There's just one assignment left to go. It's time for some chillaxing!"

With Rainbow Dash's
help, Starlight created
the perfect chillaxing
space for her friends
up on the castle roof.
"Okay, we have
sunshine, chairs,
and water," she said.
"Have I missed anything,
Rainbow Dash?"

"Just some quiet!" Rainbow Dash laughed. "And remember
that this time you can only pass your assignment by doing
absolutely nothing!"